MR. NOSEY

by Roger Hargreaves

Mr Nosey liked to know about everything that was going on.

He was always poking his nose into other people's business.

Mr Nosey was the sort of a person who, if they came upon a locked door, couldn't resist looking through the keyhole to see why the door had been locked.

Mr Nosey was the sort of a person who, if he found an unopened letter addressed to somebody else, would simply have to open it to find out what was inside.

Mr Brown,
16 High Street,
Tiddletown

Mr Nosey was the sort of a person who, if he was sitting reading his paper on a train, would much rather read the paper of the person sitting next to him.

Naturally, as you might well imagine, Mr Nosey was not very popular.

People did not like the way in which Mr Nosey would peek and pry into their affairs.

They did not like it at all, but did that stop Mr Nosey peeking and prying?

It did not!

Mr Nosey lived in a funny tall thin house in a place called Tiddletown.

The people of Tiddletown decided that Mr Nosey was becoming much too nosey, and so they held a meeting to discuss what to do about him.

"We must find some way of stopping him being so nosey," said old Mr Chips the town carpenter.

"That's right!" said Mrs Washer who ran the Tiddletown laundry. "He needs to be taught a lesson."

"If only we could think of a way to stop him poking his nose into everything," said Mr Brush the painter.

And then, a small smile spread over his face.

"Listen," he said, now grinning. "I have a plan!"

All his friends gathered round to listen to his plan.

The following morning Mr Nosey was out walking along Tiddletown High Street when he heard somebody whistling behind one of the closed doors.

"I wonder what's going on here?" he thought to himself, and tiptoeing up to the door he quietly opened it and peeped in.

"SPLASH" went a very wet paint brush right on the end of Mr Nosey's nose covering it with bright red paint.

"Oh dear. I AM sorry!" said Mr Brush, who was painting the inside of the door.

Poor Mr Nosey had to go straight home to try and remove the red paint, which was very difficult and rather painful.

Mr Brush chuckled to himself.

The Plan had begun.

The following day Mr Nosey was walking past the laundry when he heard somebody laughing on the other side of the wall.

"I wonder what's going on here?" he thought to himself, and standing on tiptoe he looked over the wall.

"SNAP" went a clothes peg right on the end of Mr Nosey's nose.

"Oh dear. I AM sorry!" said Mrs Washer, who was hanging up clothes on a washing line on the other side of the wall.

Poor Mr Nosey removed the clothes peg, and went off down the street feeling extremely sorry for himself and for his poor red nose.

Mrs Washer chuckled to herself.

The Plan was working.

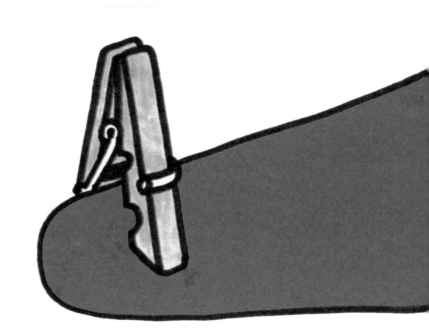

The next day Mr Nosey was going past a fence when he heard hammering.

"I wonder what's going on here?" he thought to himself, and creeping very quietly to the end of the fence he peeped round.

"BANG" went a hammer right on the end of
Mr Nosey's nose.

"Oh dear. I AM sorry!" said old Mr Chips, who was
nailing up a loose plank in the fence.

Poor Mr Nosey had to go home immediately and
bandage his poor red sore nose.

Mr Chips grinned a broad grin.

The Plan was working very well indeed.

The following day Mr Nosey was walking in the woods when he heard somebody sawing wood.

"I wonder what's going on here?" he thought to himself, and he crept up behind a tree.

He was just about to peer out from behind the tree when it suddenly occurred to him that if he did, something very nasty might happen to his nose.

And so, he went on his way without being nosey.

Behind the tree, with a saw raised in his hand, stood Mr Herd the farmer.

When he saw that Mr Nosey had gone on his way without being nosey he laughed and laughed and laughed.

The Plan had worked.

Mr Herd hurried into Tiddletown to tell everybody.

The Plan really had worked because after that Mr Nosey stopped being nosey and soon became very good friends with everybody in Tiddletown.

And that is the end of the story, except to say that if you are ever tempted to be as nosey as Mr Nosey used to be you'd better expect one thing.

A sore nose!

3 Great Offers For Mr Men Fans

1 FREE Door Hangers and Posters

In every Mr Men and Little Miss Book like this one you will find a special token. Collect 6 and we will send you either a brilliant Mr. Men or Little Miss poster and a Mr Men or Little Miss double sided, full colour, bedroom door hanger. Apply using the coupon overleaf, enclosing six tokens and a 50p coin for your choice of two items.

Egmont World tokens can be used towards any other Egmont World / World International token scheme promotions, in early learning and story / activity books.

Posters: Tick your preferred choice of either Mr Men ☐ or Little Miss ☐

Door Hangers: Choose from: Mr. Nosey & Mr Muddle ☐, Mr Greedy & Mr Lazy ☐, Mr Tickle & Mr Grumpy ☐, Mr Slow & Mr Busy ☐ Mr Messy & Mr Quiet ☐, Mr Perfect & Mr Forgetful ☐, Little Miss Fun & Little Miss Late ☐, Little Miss Helpful & Little Miss Tidy ☐, Little Miss Busy & Little Miss Brainy ☐, Little Miss Star & Little Miss Fun ☐.
(Please tick)

2 Mr Men Library Boxes

Keep your growing collection of Mr Men and Little Miss books in these superb library boxes. With an integral carrying handle and stay-closed fastener, these full colour, plastic boxes are fantastic. They are just £5.49 each including postage. Order overleaf.

3 Join The Club

To join the fantastic Mr Men & Little Miss Club, check out the page overleaf NOW!

Join Our Club!

MR.MEN & Little Miss CLUB

When you become a member of the fantastic Mr Men and Little Miss Club you'll receive a personal letter from Mr Happy and Little Miss Giggles, a club badge with your name, and a superb Welcome Pack (pictured below right).

You'll also get birthday and Christmas cards from the Mr Men and Little Misses, 2 newsletters crammed with special offers, privileges and news, and a copy of the 12 page Mr Men catalogue which includes great party ideas.

If it were on sale in the shops, the Welcome Pack alone might cost around £13. But a year's membership is just £9.99 (plus 73p postage) with a 14 day money-back guarantee if you are not delighted!

HOW TO APPLY To apply for any of these three great offers, ask an adult to complete the coupon below and send it with appropriate payment and tokens (where required) to: Mr Men Offers, PO Box 7, Manchester M19 2HD. Credit card orders for Club membership ONLY by telephone, please call: 01403 242727.

To be completed by an adult

❑ **1.** Please send a poster and door hanger as selected overleaf. I enclose six tokens and a 50p coin for post (coin not required if you are also taking up 2. or 3. below).

❑ **2.** Please send __ Mr Men Library case(s) and __ Little Miss Library case(s) at £5.49 each.

❑ **3.** Please enrol the following in the Mr Men & Little Miss Club at £10.72 (inc postage)

Fan's Name:_____Fan's Address:_____

_____Post Code:_____Date of birth:___/___/___

Your Name:_____Your Address:_____

_____

Post Code:_____Name of parent or guardian (if not you):_____

Total amount due: £_____ (£5.49 per Library Case, £10.72 per Club membership)

❑ I enclose a cheque or postal order payable to Egmont World Limited.

❑ Please charge my MasterCard / Visa account.

Card number: | | | | | | | | | | | | | | | | |

Expiry Date: _____/_____   Signature: _____

Data Protection Act: If you do **not** wish to receive other family offers from us or companies we recommend, please tick this box ❑. Offer applies to UK only